Handshake
In Space

ODYSSEY

For Fernando — S.T.

This book is dedicated to my brother,
Air Force Master Sergeant
Henry Drew Higgins, Jr., Retired — H.B.

Book copyright © 1998 Trudy Corporation, 353 Main Avenue, Norwalk, CT 06851,
and the Smithsonian Institution, Washington, DC, 20560.

Soundprints is a division of Trudy Corporation, Norwalk, Connecticut.

Book Design: Diane Hinze Kanzler

First Edition 1998
10 9 8 7 6 5 4 3 2 1
Printed in Hong Kong

Acknowledgements:
   Our very special thanks to Cathleen Lewis and Dr. Valerie Neal at the Smithsonian Institution's
National Air and Space Museum for their curatorial review.

Library of Congress Cataloging-in-Publication Data

Tan, Sheri
    Handshake in space : the Apollo-Soyuz Test Project / by Sheri Tan : illustrated by Higgins Bond.
            p.   cm. — (Odyssey)
    Summary: During a field trip to the Smithsonian's National Air and Space Museum, Lucy and
    Kevin time travel to the 1975 Apollo-Soyuz Test Project and find themselves as Alexei Leonov
    and Thomas Stafford enacting the historic first rendezvous in space.
            ISBN 1-56899-534-2 (hardcover) ISBN 1-56899-535-0 (pbk.)
            [1. Apollo-Soyuz Test Project — Fiction. 2. Time travel — Fiction. 3. School field trips —
    Fiction.]   I. Bond, Higgins, ill.   II. Title.   III. Series: Odyssey (Smithsonian Institution)
    PZ7.T16125Han 1998   97-47613
    [Fic] — dc21   CIP
                                                                                       AC

Handshake In Space

Written by Sheri Tan
Illustrated by Higgins Bond

Soundprints
Where Children Discover...

Kevin, Tomas, Lucy, and Emma are walking through Space Hall in the National Air and Space Museum in Washington, DC. "This is so cool!" Kevin says. "Maybe one day I'll go into space and meet someone from another planet!"

"Have you looked in the mirror lately, Kevin?" teases Tomas. "I think you've already met him!" Everyone laughs—even Kevin.

"Look at those space suits!" says Emma.

"I wonder what it's like to be up there, floating around—" Kevin begins to say.

"Hey, you guys," Lucy calls. "Here's the exhibit on the Apollo-Soyuz mission that our teacher was talking about. Let's go check it out."

The four friends walk over to a photograph of the three
American astronauts and two Soviet cosmonauts who were part
of the history-making space flight that took place in July, 1975.

"Stafford, Slayton, and Brand, and the cosmonauts Leonov and Kubasov." Lucy reads the names from the caption of the photograph. "It says here that this was the first time that two countries planned and carried out a trip into space together."

"Here's what the whole thing looked like when the two spacecraft joined up," says Kevin. "Hey, Lucy, come look."

But Lucy doesn't hear him. She is too caught up in what she is reading about the mission.

Suddenly, Lucy finds she is sitting down. *What's going on?* she wonders. She looks around and sees that she is in a small space that looks like the cockpit of an airplane.

Someone is sitting next to Lucy. He's dressed like an astronaut, and the name on his space suit reads KUBASOV. Lucy gasps. *That's Valeri Kubasov, the cosmonaut who was in the Soyuz space-craft with. . .* Lucy is afraid to look down at her outfit. Her heart is pounding when she sees that she is also wearing a space suit — with the name LEONOV stitched on the front.

Just then, Kubasov turns to her and smiles. Lucy smiles back, but she feels nervous. *He thinks I'm Alexei A. Leonov, the cosmonaut who led the Soviet Union in its first joint space flight with the United States!*

Lucy looks out a porthole. They have just blasted off from Baikonur Cosmodrome, and it won't be long before they meet the American Apollo crew — in space!

9

Back at the museum, Kevin cannot take his eyes off the Apollo and Soyuz spacecraft display. He wishes he could get a closer look, or better yet, be inside the Apollo spacecraft.

Suddenly, his eyes open wide. What he sees is not a display in a museum, but a spacecraft floating in what appears to be outer space. Kevin rubs his eyes. The spacecraft is still there. *Where in the world am I?* thinks Kevin.

Looking around, Kevin notices that he is wearing an astronaut's space suit — and the name STAFFORD is sewn on it! Two men are in the craft with him. Checking their name tags, Kevin sees they read SLAYTON and BRAND.

"Looking good, Tom," Vance Brand says as he glances over at Kevin.

Kevin has to keep from laughing out loud. *They think I am Thomas P. Stafford, commander of the Apollo crew!* He opens his mouth to correct Brand, then changes his mind.

"Yes, I think we're ready to dock," Kevin says, trying to sound like the spaceship commanders he's watched a thousand times on TV.

Meanwhile, Lucy watches through
a periscope as Apollo slowly moves
toward the Soviet ship.
Guided by computers, the American crew
steers Apollo toward Soyuz.
As the spacecraft get closer and closer,
Lucy's excitement increases. *I can't
wait to meet members of
the other crew,* she thinks.

In the Apollo vehicle, Kevin is thinking the same thing.

The crew members of both spacecraft are able to communicate with each other by radio transmission. On board Soyuz, Lucy hears a familiar voice being transmitted from Apollo.

"Less than five meters distance," Kevin is saying. "Three meters. . .one meter. . .contact." The two spacecraft touch.

I must really be dreaming, Lucy thinks. *That sounds like Kevin.* She shakes her head, then quickly responds to the American commander.

"We have capture," she says. The latches on both spacecraft hook and close on each other, connecting the two vehicles tightly into one giant spaceship.

"We also have capture," Kevin says. "We have succeeded. Everything is excellent."

". . .Okay, Soyuz and Apollo are shaking hands now. . ." says Lucy. "It was a good show. We're looking forward now to shaking hands with you on. . .board Soyuz."

Everyone — in both space vehicles and on earth — smiles.

"Docking is completed, Houston," Kevin says.

We did it! Lucy grins at her partner. She's glad Kubasov can't see that she has her fingers crossed.

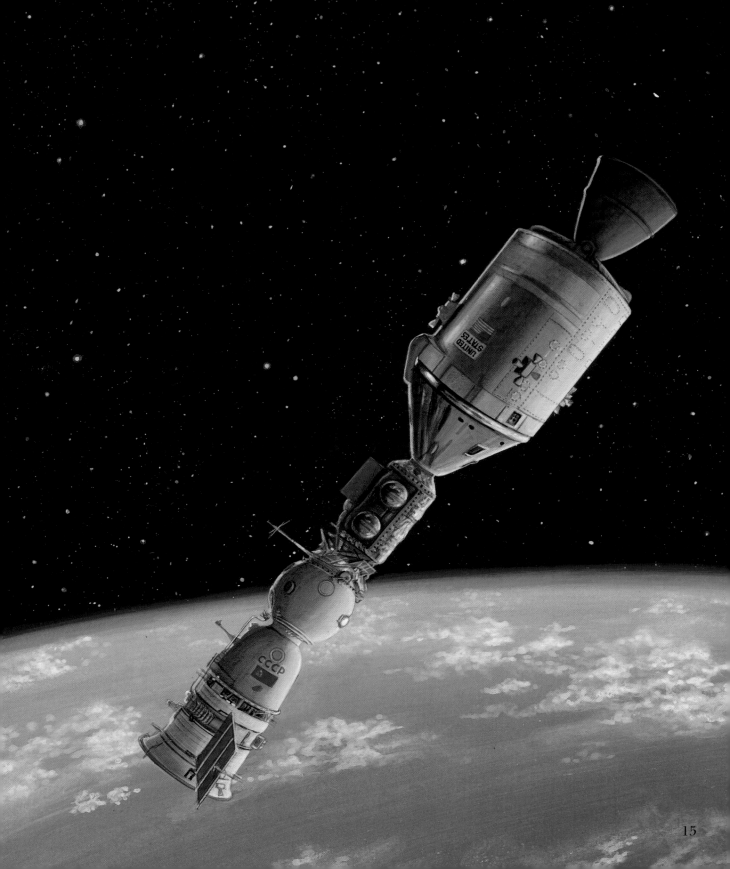

As the world watches, the astronauts and cosmonauts are finally about to meet face-to-face, 140 miles above the earth.

"Soyuz, okay to unlock?" Kevin says.

"Yes," Lucy says.

Exactly as planned, the door between the American and Soviet spacecraft swings open. Kevin reaches out to shake hands with…Lucy! Kevin and Lucy both gasp when they see each other.

"Very glad to see you, Tom," Lucy says quickly, after glancing at the name on Kevin's space suit.

"My pleasure, Alexei," says Kevin. *This is unbelievable!* he thinks, as he gives Lucy a big smile.

In Washington, DC, President Gerald R. Ford has been watching this historic event on TV and is ready to congratulate the members of both the American and Soviet crews. His message is transmitted to both ships.

"…Let me call you to express my very great admiration for your hard work, your total dedication in preparing for this first joint flight," President Ford says. "All of us here in…the United States send to you our very warmest congratulations for your successful rendezvous and for your docking and we wish you the very best for a successful completion of the remainder of your mission.…It has taken us many years to open this door to useful cooperation in space between our two countries."

Kevin feels a sense of pride as he hears the president's voice. *What an honor!* he thinks.

When Kevin enters the Soyuz spacecraft, he is greeted by a banner that says, "Welcome aboard Soyuz."

The Soviets host the first dinner in space. Kevin joins Lucy and Kubasov for a dinner of borscht (a traditional Russian soup made with beets), jellied turkey, cheese, and small loaves of black bread.

During the mission, the astronauts and cosmonauts share several meals together. Sometimes they eat in Soyuz and sometimes in Apollo.

"How do you like American food?" a reporter asks Lucy, after one of the meals in Apollo.

"Space food is not the same food eaten by people on earth," she replies. Then, remembering something that her grandfather had told her, Lucy adds, "But as an old philosopher says, 'The best part of a good dinner is not what you eat, but with whom you eat.' Today I have dinner together with my very good friends, Tom Stafford and Deke Slayton.…it was the best part of my dinner."

Kevin reaches over to shake Lucy's hand. "You said that well," he says.

On each spacecraft, there are gifts that the two crews exchange to celebrate this important mission.

Each team has brought with them halves of two plaques and two medallions. They join the halves to make one set for each crew to take home. The Soviets and the Americans also exchange tree seeds, to be planted in each other's homeland so that the memory of the mission will never go away. Then they also present each other with flags, and the Americans give their new friends books by the American rocket scientist Robert Goddard. In return, the Soviets present the American crew with the works of Russian rocket pioneer Konstantin E. Tsiolkovski.

Members of both crews sign a certificate issued by the *Federation Aeronautique Internationale* that makes this trip official in the record books.

Kevin uses his neatest handwriting as he signs the name "Thomas P. Stafford" on the certificate.

I can do it, Lucy says to herself when it is her turn to sign. Carefully, in Russian letters, she writes "Alexei A. Leonov," then gives the pen to cosmonaut Kubasov.

Whew! she sighs. It looks just fine.

To remember this mission, Lucy decides to draw the astronauts and cosmonauts at work in the spacecraft. She holds up a sketch to the television camera so that people on earth can see what she sees!

A reporter asks her to show a picture that would be the best example of what the whole mission is about. She holds up a flag of the Soviet Union next to the American flag that Kevin is holding up. It is a picture that people all over the world will remember for a long time.

After almost two days, the joint mission has been completed. "See you on earth," Kevin says to Lucy, just before closing the hatch.

"Hey, Kevin, hurry up," Tomas calls out. "You just missed a really cool film about the space mission."

Kevin doesn't answer him. His eyes are still focused on the Apollo and Soyuz spacecraft.

"Earth to Kevin," says Emma. "Do you read me?"

"What?" Kevin says. He touches his arms and legs. He's not wearing a space suit anymore!

"What's wrong, Kevin?" asks Tomas. "Did you meet a space alien or something?"

"Very funny," Kevin says. "Where's Lucy?"

"We left her by the picture of the astronauts," says Emma.

"Lucy, Lucy!" Emma says, tugging at Lucy's sleeve when they find her. "Don't tell me you're in outer space, too!"

"Uh, *nyet*…I mean, no," Lucy says. "I, uh, was just wondering if there's an exhibit like this in Russia."

Lucy looks around quickly — she is no longer in the Soyuz spacecraft, and Kevin is standing beside her!

"Hey, Leonov, did you enjoy your trip into space?" Kevin whispers to Lucy, as they go through the doors of the museum.

"Yes," says Lucy, "but I feel really hungry for some reason."

"I could use some earth food now, myself," replies Kevin, laughing as they high-five each other. "Space travel is hard work!"

About the Apollo-Soyuz Mission

In the 1970s, the United States and the Soviet Union were the only two nations with established space-flight programs sending humans into space. These countries were not then friendly with each other. In fact, they were rivals in a power struggle called the Cold War. So, it was very meaningful that in 1972, President Richard M. Nixon and Soviet Prime Minister Alexei Kosygin signed an agreement to work on a joint space mission, officially called the Apollo-Soyuz Test Project. Many doubted that the mission could take place because of the difference in political beliefs. They worried because the two countries would have to share technological information that could be used against each other.

The goal of the project was to show that it was possible for two orbiting spacecraft to join together. A successful flight would mean further exchange of ideas and information about space between the two countries, and cooperation setting up rescue strategies to help spacecraft in trouble. The mission would be a first step toward an international earth-orbiting space station, where people from different countries could live and work together in space.

Nine American astronauts and eight Soviet cosmonauts — as well as many scientists and engineers — spent three years preparing for the mission. The American space crew studied and spoke the Russian language and the cosmonauts studied and spoke English. While the two vehicles were connected in space, the crews sometimes spoke Russian together, and sometimes English.

The Apollo spacecraft was launched from Cape Canaveral in Florida, and the Soyuz spacecraft took off from Baikonur Cosmodrome, about 2000 miles from Moscow. Shortly after noon, Houston time, on July 17, 1975, the two vessels docked together. About two hours later, the historic handshake between astronaut Thomas P. Stafford and cosmonaut Alexei A. Leonov took place. The simple handshake between an American and a Soviet represented the hope that all countries could set aside their differences and work together for the common good of the world.

Linked together, the Apollo-Soyuz pair was 66 feet long and weighed 47,500 pounds. It looked like an odd-shaped barbell. The total time that the two ships were connected was 46 hours and 46 minutes, almost two full days.

Many major world events have occurred since that mission in 1975. The Soviet Union is no longer a country — but in today's Russia, the established space program continues. The goals of the original space programs have also changed, but the US and Russia continue learning from each other, and are currently working on missions similar to the Apollo-Soyuz Test Project. The first in a series of dockings of the US Space Shuttle with the Russian space station Mir took place in 1995, twenty years after astronaut Stafford and cosmonaut Leonov first shook hands in space.

Glossary

astronaut: a person trained for space flight

capture: the touching and latching together of two spacecraft

cosmodrome: the Russian term for a launch site for space missions

cosmonaut: the Russian term for astronaut

Federation Aeronautique Internationale: International Federation of Aeronautics; an international aeronautics league

Houston: a city in Texas where NASA's mission control center is located

mission: work that one is sent to do — in this case a space-flight, including all tasks done for it in space and preparing for it on the ground

NASA: the initials, or acronym, for the National Aeronautics and Space Administration

periscope: a tube with a mirror or prism at each end that makes it possible to see around or past something that blocks normal vision

pioneer: a person who is among the first to explore a place or field of study

rendezvous: in spaceflight, a close approach of two or more spacecraft without actual contact